Dear Parents and Educators,

Welcome to Penguin Young Readers! As parents and educators, you know that each child develops at his or her own pace—in terms of speech, critical thinking, and, of course, reading. Penguin Young Readers recognizes this fact. As a result, each Penguin Young Readers book is assigned a traditional easy-to-read level (1–4) as well as a Guided Reading Level (A–P). Both of these systems will help you choose the right book for your child. Please refer to the back of each book for specific leveling information. Penguin Young Readers features esteemed authors and illustrators, stories about favorite characters, fascinating nonfiction, and more!

The Bookstore Valentine

LEVEL **3**

GUIDED READING LEVEL **J**

This book is perfect for a **Transitional Reader** who:
- can read multisyllable and compound words;
- can read words with prefixes and suffixes;
- is able to identify story elements (beginning, middle, end, plot, setting, characters, problem, solution); and
- can understand different points of view.

Here are some **activities** you can do during and after reading this book:
- Compound Words: A compound word is made when two words are joined together to form a new word. First look for the following compound words in the story: bookstore, cobweb, sweetheart, upstairs, downstairs, bookcase. Then, on a separate sheet of paper, write down the definition for each compound word. Next, break each word into two separate words and write down the meaning for each word.
- Chapter Titles: The title of each chapter is very important. It should catch the reader's attention, and it should say something about what happens. The four chapters in this book do not have titles. Work with the child to come up with titles based on what happens in each chapter.

Remember, sharing the love of reading with a child is the best gift you can give!

—Bonnie Bader, EdM
  Penguin Young Readers program

*Penguin Young Readers are leveled by independent reviewers applying the standards developed by Irene Fountas and Gay Su Pinnell in *Matching Books to Readers: Using Leveled Books in Guided Reading*, Heinemann, 1999.

For Nancy—BM

For Mary Schullo and her students—DL

Penguin Young Readers
Published by the Penguin Group
Penguin Group (USA) Inc., 375 Hudson Street, New York, New York 10014, USA
Penguin Group (Canada), 90 Eglinton Avenue East, Suite 700, Toronto, Ontario M4P 2Y3, Canada
(a division of Pearson Penguin Canada Inc.)
Penguin Books Ltd, 80 Strand, London WC2R 0RL, England
Penguin Ireland, 25 St Stephen's Green, Dublin 2, Ireland (a division of Penguin Books Ltd)
Penguin Group (Australia), 707 Collins Street, Melbourne, Victoria 3008, Australia
(a division of Pearson Australia Group Pty Ltd)
Penguin Books India Pvt Ltd, 11 Community Centre, Panchsheel Park, New Delhi—110 017, India
Penguin Group (NZ), 67 Apollo Drive, Rosedale, Auckland 0632, New Zealand
(a division of Pearson New Zealand Ltd)
Penguin Books (South Africa), Rosebank Office Park, 181 Jan Smuts Avenue,
Parktown North 2193, South Africa
Penguin China, B7 Jiaming Center, 27 East Third Ring Road North,
Chaoyang District, Beijing 100020, China

Penguin Books Ltd, Registered Offices: 80 Strand, London WC2R 0RL, England

Text copyright © 2002 by Barbara Maitland. Illustrations copyright © 2002 by David LaRochelle.
All rights reserved. First published in 2002 by Puffin Books and Dutton Children's Books, imprints of
Penguin Group (USA) Inc. Published in 2013 by Penguin Young Readers, an imprint of
Penguin Group (USA) Inc., 345 Hudson Street, New York, New York 10014. Manufactured in China.

The Library of Congress has cataloged the Dutton edition
under the following Control Number: 2003274240

ISBN 978-0-14-230187-6   10 9 8 7 6 5 4 3 2 1

ALWAYS LEARNING   PEARSON

PENGUIN YOUNG READERS

LEVEL
TRANSITIONAL
READER
3

THE BOOKSTORE VALENTINE

by Barbara Maitland
illustrated by David LaRochelle

Penguin Young Readers
An Imprint of Penguin Group (USA) Inc.

Chapter 1

Mr. Brown loved his store.

It was called the

Black Cat Bookstore.

The Black Cat Bookstore sold

only ghost books.

And it had a ghost!

Mr. Brown loved his cat, too.

Her name was Cobweb.

Cobweb was different from other cats.

She ate only cheese.

And she liked to play with mice!

BLACK CAT BOOKSTORE

Mr. Brown and Cobweb lived
above the store.
They always ate cheese
for breakfast.
And they always opened
the store together.

7

One morning Mr. Brown said,

"Valentine's Day is coming.

I will have a sale."

He put a sign in the window.

People saw the sign.

They came into the store and

crowded around Mr. Brown.

"There are only four days until

Valentine's Day," they said.

"We need to buy gifts."

"Do you have *The Haunted Honeymoon?*"

"Do you have *My Spooky Sweetheart?*"

"Can you gift wrap *My Boo-tiful Ghost?*"

"One at a time, please!" said Mr. Brown.

The store grew more and more crowded.

CRASH! Books fell on the floor.

Sometimes people dropped them.

Sometimes the ghost did.

Mr. Brown was very busy.

He could not pick them up.

SPOOKTACULAR
LOVE
STORIES

13

That night Mr. Brown was tired.

"Valentine's Day is coming,"

he told Cobweb.

"The store is so busy.

I need help!"

He put a new sign in the window:

It said: HELP WANTED!

Then he and Cobweb
went upstairs to bed.

Chapter 2

The next morning
Mr. Brown got up early.
He made some cheese snacks.

Then he and Cobweb went down
to the store.

A woman was waiting outside.

Mr. Brown let her in.

"My name is Miss Button,"
the woman said.

"I saw your sign.

I like ghost books.

I would like the job."

"Good," said Mr. Brown.

"Welcome to Black Cat Bookstore.

We have ghost books and a ghost."

He held out the cheese.

"Would you like some cheese?"

"Oh, I love cheese," said Miss Button.

Cobweb jumped up beside Miss Button.

"This is my cat, Cobweb," said Mr. Brown.

CRASH! A book fell off a shelf.

"And that was my ghost.

It is special!"

"Wonderful!" said Miss Button.

"I like cats.

I like ghosts, too!"

"You are perfect!" said Mr. Brown.

He blushed.

"For the job, I mean."

They got to work.

Mr. Brown sold books.

He smiled when he saw Miss Button.

Miss Button cut out some paper hearts.

She put them up all over the store.

She smiled when she saw Mr. Brown.

THE
GRUESOME
TWOSOME

Miss Button was putting up hearts

in the window when . . .

Crash! A book fell beside her.

"Aha!" she said to the mice.

"So you are the ghost.

How clever of you."

At the end of the day, Miss Button said,

"I have enjoyed my day."

"I have enjoyed my day, too,"

said Mr. Brown.

"I think they like each other,"

Cobweb told the mice.

Chapter 3

The next day, Mr. Brown put balloons
around the store.

He thought about Miss Button.

"Perfect!" he said to himself.

Miss Button sold books.

She thought about Mr. Brown.

"Wonderful!" she said to herself.

At the end of the next day,

Mr. Brown said,

"Miss Button?

Tomorrow is Valentine's Day.

I was wondering if . . ."

"Yes?" said Miss Button.

Mr. Brown turned red.

"*Ummm* . . . nothing.

I'll see you in the morning."

On Valentine's Day morning,

Mr. Brown went downstairs early.

He took a paper heart from his pocket.

He wrote on it.

MISS BUTTON,
PLEASE HAVE DINNER
WITH ME TONIGHT.
LOVE,
NORRIS
BROWN

He sighed.

"What if she says no?"

he asked Cobweb.

He dropped the heart in the trash can.

Mr. Brown was selling books when
Miss Button arrived.

She hung up her coat.

She took a paper heart from her bag.

She wrote on it.

Mr. Brown,
Please have dinner
with me tonight.
Love,
Emily Button

She sighed.

"What if he says no?" she asked the mice.

She left the heart on a shelf.

Miss Button went to help Mr. Brown.

Cobweb dipped her paw

in the trash can.

She fished out Mr. Brown's note.

The mice took Miss Button's note

from the shelf.

They carried it to Cobweb.

"They are too shy to send these notes,"

said the mice.

"Maybe we can help," said Cobweb.

"I have a plan."

Chapter 4

Cobweb walked over to Mr. Brown
and Miss Button.

She jumped onto a bookcase.

She dropped a note in front of

Mr. Brown.

The mice dropped the other note.

It fell right in front of Miss Button.

Mr. Brown and Miss Button
picked up the notes.
They both read them out loud:
"Please have dinner
with me tonight."

"Dinner would be wonderful,"
said Miss Button.

"Perfect!" said Mr. Brown.

At the end of the day, Miss Button
and Mr. Brown went upstairs.
Miss Button made hearts
out of string cheese.
Mr. Brown made cheese pizza
and cheesecake.

Then they went back downstairs
to the bookstore.

Miss Button lit candles.

Mr. Brown put out the food.

"Can Cobweb and your ghost come
to dinner, too?" asked Miss Button.

"Ahem," said Mr. Brown.

"About my ghost . . ."

"Don't worry, Norris," said Miss Button.

"I like mice."

"Emily, you *are* perfect!"

said Mr. Brown.

They all sat together.

Mr. Brown raised his glass.

"To ghosts, Cobweb, and my
bookstore Valentine," he said.